Deer Song

By Jay VandeVoorde

Illustrated by Joe Tallent

AuthorHouse™
1663 Liberty Drive, Suite 200
Bloomington, IN 47403
www.authorhouse.com
Phone: 1-800-839-8640

AuthorHouse™ UK Ltd.
500 Avebury Boulevard
Central Milton Keynes, MK9 2BE
www.authorhouse.co.uk
Phone: 08001974150

First published by AuthorHouse 2/24/2006

Summary: John is a hunter in search of the perfect deer. He spends many hours preparing his camp in Northern Michigan; however, John soon realizes that the deer in the woods has more to offer than to simply be his prey. Through his love of music, John develops a love for compassion.

ISBN: 1-4259-2027-6

Library of Congress Control Number: 2006901595

Printed in the United States of America
Bloomington, Indiana

This book is printed on acid-free paper.

Jay VandeVoorde's photo used by permission of Lifetouch National School Studios, Comstock Park, Michigan.

Joe Tallent's photo used by permission of Paris Studios, Muskegon, Michigan.

Bloomington, IN Milton Keynes, UK

authorHOUSE

Author's Dedication:

To Mom and Pebbles for their tremendous support. To Joe, my illustrator, for his hard work and dedication in making this book a success.

Illustrator's Dedication:

To my loving family who never doubts me and to my wonderful mentors, Mrs. Versraete and Mrs. Benson-Fennell. To the Coca Cola Company for the many hours of late night drawing. Special thanks to Jay for never giving up on me.

One cool autumn morning in a Great Lakes forest, John Doe woke up before dawn at his hunting cabin which overlooked a crystal-clear lake.

John Doe was a big man. He had long red hair and stood as tall as a Michigan pine tree. John had whiskers that were unkept and a strawberry shaped nose. He smelled like the outdoors itself. Today he got dressed in his warm autumn clothes and made himself a hunter's breakfast of bacon and eggs, topped off with a piping hot cup of coffee.

He grabbed his ax, some rope, and his radio and trudged off, whistling a melody of songs. It was a long hike, but John enjoyed every moment in the serene sun-dappled forest of white pines and yellow birch trees.

John decided to rest a moment before starting to build his deer blind. Playing the sweet sounds of his favorite country music on the radio he relaxed in the shade of the tree where his blind was to be built.

Suddenly, John had
an eerie feeling that he was
being watched. He searched
the field and saw nothing.
Slowly he turned his head
and there in the field was
one of the most beautiful
does he had ever seen.

The only sound was the soft melodies from the radio as the two stared at each other. Both hunter and prey remained motionless as time seemed to stand still.

The music on the radio abruptly ended and turned into the news of the day. The deer bolted with the change and disappeared into the forest before John could blink an eye.

John sighed. But, it was time to get to work anyway.

That evening as John hiked back to his cabin, and later when he ate his dinner and watched the woods grow dark, his mind recalled the beautiful deer he'd seen so distinctly. He wondered if she would visit on opening day when he had his rifle.

John opened his eyes in the morning just as the birds started singing.

Before starting work he headed out to his picnic table to feel the warmth of the morning sun on his tall body. He turned on his radio and breathed in deeply, enjoying the fresh forest scent and clean country air.

John sat bolt upright. Again, he had the strange feeling of being watched! There, on the footpath into the forest, stood a doe. There was no doubt in John's mind it was the same deer he had spotted the day before.

Slowly, the deer began to approach John who was sitting quietly at the picnic table. On the table was a basket of apples that he had brought to munch on.

The radio continued to play softly in the background. John thought he should turn it off to keep the deer close by. However, when he flicked off the switch she bolted and ran for the nearest brush. John sat at the picnic table in deep thought. Could it be possible? Did the deer come around because of the soothing sound of music?

He turned the radio back on and waited. It didn't take long and she was back.

Amazingly, after a short time, the deer lay close to John and the picnic table.   The
hunter and the prey sat most of the morning as he formulated an idea in his head.

Tomorrow was the opening day of deer hunting season. All he would have to do is turn on the radio and wait for his prize to show up at his cabin. Then POW, he'd have his deer!

With that thought John turned off the radio and the deer scrambled up and ran away.

John couldn't sleep that night. He wasn't a patient man and his idea kept him up most of the night.

The next
m o r n i n g
at dawn John
turned on his
radio and let the
music spread through
the forest.

Sure enough, the doe appeared a
short time later from the path in the forest. She
moved toward the hunter in a more calm and sure manner
than before, and John knew she was trusting him for more
apples.   John moved his gun, slowly and gradually, toward his
shoulder and took aim at his deer. He could hear his heart beating and he
had trouble holding the gun steady.

The doe watched him in a curious, and John thought, friendly way.

He placed his finger on the trigger. With just the sound of music from the radio, the hunter and the deer looked at each other. The seconds seemed like hours, until……

.........THUMP! An apple hit the ground. John Doe had a change of heart and he couldn't kill the beautiful doe.

28

The doe started munching on the apple right alongside the hunter. John and the deer
spent the rest of the morning eating apples and listening to their favorite music.
In fact, that's what they both did for the rest of the deer hunting season.

Some people say that if you listen closely when you're in a forest around the Great Lakes you might hear the sound of soft music playing.

And if you follow that sound, you're sure to find John Doe and his deer listening to their favorite music and eating apples----sharing good times, just as good friends should.

Jay Vande Voorde was born and raised in Muskegon, Michigan. Jay is a graduate of Muskegon Catholic Central, Muskegon Community College, and Central Michigan University. He is presently an Instructional Coach for the Muskegon Heights Public Schools. He enjoys the outdoors, gardening, reading, and traveling. He has traveled extensively throughout Europe. He also has a passion for hockey and is in the process of writing History of Hockey in Muskegon.

Joe Tallent lives in Muskegon with his loving family and is in his senior year at Mona Shores High School. Joe spends his time in art and would love to pursue being an art instructor. From designing his high school mascot to spending his summer drawing portraits at Cedar Fair Amusement Parks, Joe keeps very busy.